Eva

spreads love wherev...

by Suzanne
Marshall

LiveWellMedia.com

ISBN-13: 978-1539072201
ISBN-10: 1539072207

NOTE TO PARENTS

In this story, **Eva** can be whomever your child relates to the most. The illustrations are meant to reflect the wonderful diversity in America (and the world) and to deliver a message about the power of love and unity. While we would love to portray *all* children within these pages, the richness of our world's diversity makes that an impossible task for this book.

This book is dedicated to

Eva

who is loved very much!

On beautiful days under the sun,
Eva plays with her chums.

Eva and her friends
are different from each other,
but just like notes in a joyful song,
they come together and get along.

They've got a lot in common too.
They like fresh air and skies of blue,
and dogs that bark and cats that mew,
and birds that sing a song or two.
They like to whoop and say: "Yahoo!"

One day a bellowing beast stomps by.
He acts like a bully. So the children hide.

His words are like flames burning their ears,
making them nervous, making them scared.

Eva and her friends run away
and find a park where they can play.
Eva relaxes once again,
romping around with her friends.

But soon
the beast
reappears,
stirring anxiety,
stirring fear.

The beast has nothing good to say.
His words cause nothing but dismay.

Eva and her friends run away
and find a farm where they can play.
Among the chickens, Eva smiles.
She even forgets the beast for a while.

But who do you think
appears on the scene?

Who do you think
is obnoxious and mean?

The beast shows up with poisonous words,
spewing things that should never be heard.

Eva and her friends run away
and find a stream where they can play.

Among the turtles, ducks and geese,
Eva sighs with deep relief.

She and her friends enjoy the peace.
They grin and giggle and laugh with ease.

But guess who comes
and ruins their fun?

The beast insults them
one by one.

You'd think he'd get tired of making jeers,
but the more he shouts, the less he hears.
He hasn't heard anything new for years!

Eva and her friends run away
and find a tree where they can play.
In the shade, they gather together.
Beneath the branches, they feel better.

Eva wants to be happy.
She wants to be kind.
But she has got a lot on her mind.
She can't forget the beast this time.

When the beast shows up,
as she knows he will,
Eva doesn't run.
No, she's very still.

Eva says:
"We must be brave. We must be strong.
We must unite and act as one.
If we speak up, steady and clear,
the voice of the beast
will be harder to hear."

As Eva lifts her voice in the air,
her friends join in with a cheer.

The beast tries to interfere,
but soon his voice disappears.

Eva and her friends
say loving words
till only the sound
of love is heard.

Eva and her friends
are true heroes,
spreading love
wherever they go.

Love spreads
from here to there,
word by word,
everywhere!

Acknowledgements

I am very grateful for my extraordinary editorial team: Rachel and Hannah Roeder, and Don Marshall. Special thanks to Joan McKniff and Nathaniel Robinson for their valuable input, and to all who have supported my creative journey including my mom and dad.

Illustrations have been edited by the author. *Original children and most scenes: © Bluering/Fotosearch.com. Island/boat: © Colematt. Original beast: © RaStudio/Fotosearch. Additional elements were curated from freekpik.com.*

About the Author

An honors graduate of Smith College, Suzanne Marshall writes to inspire, engage and empower children. Learn more about Suzanne and her books at **LiveWellMedia.com.** *(Photo: Suzanne & Abby Underdog)*

19685172R00023

Printed in Poland
by Amazon Fulfillment
Poland Sp. z o.o., Wrocław